# The Secret Garden

*Retold from the Frances Hodgson Burnett*
*original by Martha Hailey*

*Illustrated by Lucy Corvino*

STERLING CHILDREN'S BOOKS

New York

## STERLING CHILDREN'S BOOKS
New York

An Imprint of Sterling Publishing Co., Inc.
1166 Avenue of the Americas
New York, NY 10036

ISBN 978-1-4027-9466-7

### Library of Congress Cataloging-in-Publication Data

Hailey, Martha.
  The secret garden / abridged by Martha Hailey; illustrated by Lucy Corvino; retold from the
original author, Frances Hodgson Burnett.
      p. cm.—(Classic starts)
  Summary: An abridged version of the tale of ten-year-old Mary who, after the death of
her parents, comes to live in a lonely house on the Yorkshire moors where she discovers an
invalid cousin and the mysteries of a locked garden.
  ISBN 1-4027-1319-3
  [1. Orphans—Fiction. 2. Gardens—Fiction. 3. People with disabilities—Fiction. 4. Yorkshire
(England)—History—20th century—Fiction. 5. Great Britain—History—Edward VII, 1901–
1910—Fiction.] I. Corvino, Lucy, ill. II. Burnett, Frances Hodgson, 1849–1924.
Secret garden. III. Title. IV. Series.
PZ7.D8542Se 2004
[Fic]—dc22
                                                                                    2004013669

Distributed in Canada by Sterling Publishing Co., Inc.
c/o Canadian Manda Group, 664 Annette Street
Toronto, Ontario M6S 2C8, Canada
Distributed in the United Kingdom by GMC Distribution Services
Castle Place, 166 High Street, Lewes, East Sussex BN7 1XU, England
Distributed in Australia by NewSouth Books
University of New South Wales, Sydney, NSW 2052, Australia

For information about custom editions, special sales, and premium and corporate purchases,
please contact Sterling Special Sales at 800-805-5489 or specialsales@sterlingpublishing.com.

Manufactured in China

Lot#:
4  6  8  10  9  7  5  3
06/19

sterlingpublishing.com

Design by Renato Stanisic
Cover illustration by Lucy Corvino

# CONTENTS

# CHAPTER 1

## No One Left

When Mary Lennox was born, no one really wanted her. Her father worked for the British government in India and had no time for raising a child. Mary's beautiful mother hadn't wanted a little girl at all; she cared only about going to parties.

So their sickly, fretful baby was handed over to an Ayah—an Indian nanny. Mary's Ayah knew that the baby's crying made her mother angry, so to keep Mary quiet, she let her have her own way in everything.

Mary grew up as selfish a child as had ever

lived. Her thin face looked yellow, and her expression was sour as a lemon. Even her blond hair wouldn't behave.

Governesses were hired to teach the cross child to read and write, but they never lasted longer than a few months. Except for her Ayah and the servants, Mary hardly ever saw other people—not even her mother.

One blazing hot morning when Mary was nine, she was awakened by an unknown servant. She wanted her Ayah, but her Ayah couldn't come. Even when Mary had a tantrum, the servant just looked frightened and repeated her message.

Mary knew something strange was happening, but no one would tell her what. Left alone, she went outside to play under a tree near the veranda. She was making a pretend flowerbed when she heard her mother's voice speaking with a young army officer. They didn't notice the little girl, but Mary saw that her mother was alarmed.

"Is it so very bad?" her mother asked.

"Awfully," the officer replied. "You should have left two weeks ago, Mrs. Lennox, instead of staying for the ball."

Just then, Mary heard a shout from the servants' quarters that grew louder and wilder.

"Someone has died," the officer said, his voice shaking.

Mary's mother gasped and ran inside.

Later Mary found out that a dread disease—cholera—had broken out. Her Ayah had been the first to die, and many others were in danger. In a panic, many of the servants ran away in terror, leaving no one to care for Mary.

For two whole days, Mary hid in the nursery. Off and on, she cried and slept. She could hear odd, frightening sounds in the house and from the servants' huts. In the confusion, everyone had forgotten about her.

The next day, Mary wandered into the dining room and ate some biscuits and fruit. She also drank a glass of tonic someone had left on the table. It was like medicine, and it made her drowsy. She went back to her bedroom and fell into a deep sleep.

Mary finally awoke to silence and lay on her bed and listened for noises, but the house was perfectly still. Then she heard a rustling on the floor mat. Looking down, she saw a little snake. She wasn't afraid of him, knowing he was harmless. She watched him glide across the floor and slip under her door. Were they alone in the house? she wondered.

Then she heard heavy footsteps on the veranda and men talking in low voices. One man said, "What a shame! That beautiful woman dead! I heard there was a child, too, but no one ever saw her."

Just then, Mary's door opened. Mary stood up

and an army officer came in, looking weary and troubled. Stiffly, the child said in a cross voice, "I am Mary Lennox. I fell asleep when everyone had cholera, and I just woke up." Stamping her foot, she demanded, "Why have they forgotten me? Why does nobody come?"

A younger soldier with the officer just shook his head sadly and held Mary's hand. "Poor little kid. There's nobody left to come!"

This was the strange, sudden way Mary found out that both her parents and most of the servants had died. There really was no one left but herself and the rustling little snake.

# CHAPTER 2

## On the Moors

The soldiers took Mary to the home of the Reverend Crawford, a poor English minister. He told her that she would soon be sailing to London and would live with her guardian, Mr. Archibald Craven, at Misselthwaite Manor in Yorkshire.

So Mary left India and sailed on the long ocean voyage to England. In London, she was handed over to Mr. Craven's housekeeper, Mrs. Medlock, a stout woman with sharp black eyes and a black cape. Mary didn't like her, but then again, she hardly liked anyone.

The next day, they began their railway journey to Misselthwaite Manor. Mary sat with her hands folded in her lap and stared out the window. She pretended not to care as Mrs. Medlock told her about her new home.

"It's a grand place, in a gloomy way," the housekeeper said. "Six hundred years old, with nearly a hundred rooms full of fine paintings and furniture. But most of them are locked up. The manor's on the edge of the moor. It has a big park with gardens and trees. Do you know anything about your uncle?"

"No," Mary said, acting bored.

"But don't you care? Didn't your parents ever tell you?" Mrs. Medlock asked.

"Why should it matter?" Mary replied.

"Well, I suppose it doesn't," Mrs. Medlock said. "*He's* not going to bother about you. He never troubles himself about anyone . . ." She trailed off. A few moments later, she continued.

"Mr. Craven's got a crooked back. He was never happy till he married. His wife, your aunt, was a sweet, pretty thing, and he'd have walked the world over to get her a blade of grass if she'd asked. Some people said she married him for his money, but she didn't. When she died, he became stranger than ever—won't see people. Most times, he's away. When he's at home, he shuts himself up in the west wing. Don't expect to see him," Mrs. Medlock warned. "And don't expect people to talk to you. You'll look after yourself. You'll be told which rooms you can go into. You can play in the garden, but don't go poking about the house—Mr. Craven won't have it."

"I won't," Mary said tartly.

She turned again to look out the window. Her eyelids grew heavy looking at the gray, rainy drizzle, and she fell asleep.

A few hours later, Mrs. Medlock shook Mary. "Wake up!" she said. "We're at Thwaite Station. Now we have a long drive across Missel Moor."

Mary stood and tried to keep her eyes open. She followed Mrs. Medlock from the train onto the railway platform.

A large carriage awaited them. A footman in a long raincoat helped Mary and Mrs. Medlock inside. Then he climbed up to his seat beside the carriage driver, and they were off.

In the light of the carriage's lamps, Mary caught glimpses of the tiny village of Thwaite— whitewashed houses, a church, and a few shops. After that, she saw only trees and hedges beside the road. Then there was nothing but blackness out the carriage windows on both sides.

Suddenly she felt a sharp jolt.

"We're on the moor now!" Mrs. Medlock exclaimed.

The yellow light of the carriage lamps revealed some bushes and low-growing things along the road. In the darkness, the wind made an eerie, low, rushing sound.

"Is it the sea?" Mary asked.

"No, not the sea, or fields, or mountains," answered Mrs. Medlock mysteriously. "The moor is just miles and miles of wasteland, and no one lives on it except wild ponies and sheep." Mrs. Medlock paused. "I think it's a dreary place, but some people like it in springtime."

The carriage rattled over bridges and bumps. Mary could hear water rushing very fast under them. She felt like they were driving over a windy black ocean.

"I don't like the moor," she thought. "I don't like it at all!"

At last the carriage stopped in a clearing in front of a very long house built around a court-yard. A single light glowed from an upstairs window.

Mary followed Mrs. Medlock to a huge oak door that opened into an enormous hall with a stone floor. In the dim light, Mary could make out

portraits on the walls and figures in suits of armor. She felt very small and lost in the shadowy hall.

A thin old butler was there to meet them, but he didn't speak to Mary. The man said to Mrs. Medlock, "Mr. Craven doesn't want to see her. He's going to London in the morning and doesn't want to be disturbed."

"Very well," Mrs. Medlock replied. "I can manage."

The housekeeper led Mary up a wide staircase and down a dim hallway. Finally, they reached Mary's rooms. A coal fire burned in the hearth, and a table was set with supper.

"You can eat now. Then I'll help you get to bed," Mrs. Medlock said. "You'll have this room and the nursery next door. So don't go wandering around the house. Understand?" Mary understood, but she had perhaps never felt so miserable in her life.

# CHAPTER 3

# A Maid Named Martha

∽

Mary awoke to the sounds of a young house-maid kneeling at the fireplace, sweeping cold cinders into a pan. Mary watched her for a few moments. Then she glanced around the room.

Even in the daylight it seemed oddly gloomy. The walls were covered with a tapestry embroidered with pictures of a forest and people in strange clothing.

Mary turned to the window. She saw a great stretch of flat, treeless land. It resembled a dull purple sea.

"What's that?" she asked, pointing toward the window.

The young maid said, "That's the moor. Do you like it?"

"No," Mary said. "I hate it."

The maid grinned and said, "You'll get used to it. It looks bare in winter, but in the summer it's covered with wild heather and smells sweet as honey. The air's so fresh and the sky looks so high, full of bees and skylarks. I wouldn't live away from the moor for anything!"

Mary was puzzled. In India, the servants never talked so freely.

Curious, Mary said, "You're a strange servant. What's your name?"

The maid laughed. "I'm Martha, and I know I seem strange to you. I'm a country girl from Yorkshire. If Misselthwaite were like other big houses, I'd have to work in the kitchen. But this house has no mistress, and Mr. Craven's nearly always away, so I work upstairs."

"Are you my servant?" Mary asked.

"I'm Mrs. Medlock's servant," Martha replied, "but I'll clean your room and wait on you a bit."

Mary had to listen as Martha, whose friendly voice had a soothing effect, told her all about her large family and their cottage on the moor. "My brother Dickon is twelve, and he's got a young pony. He found it and its mother on the moor. He'd give it bits of bread and grass, and it got to like him. Now it follows him around and even lets him ride it. Dickon's a kind lad, and animals like him."

Mary began to take a slight interest in Dickon. This was strange because Mary had never been interested in anyone but herself.

Mary had some tea and a little toast. Then Martha cleared the table. "You wrap up warm and go outside to play," she said. "That will give you an appetite."

Mary looked out the window.

"Why should I go out on a day like this?" she asked. Everything looked gray and wintry.

Martha answered, "If you don't go out, you'll have to stay in. And what will you do here?"

Martha was right. There were no toys or books in the nursery or in the bedroom.

"Who will go with me?" Mary asked.

"You'll go by yourself, of course," Martha said. "Our Dickon plays on the moor alone for hours. He plays with the pony and the sheep that know him. The birds come to eat out of his hand."

Mary thought that at least there would be birds to amuse her. Martha helped her into her coat, cap, and sturdy boots, and led her downstairs. At the door, Martha pointed to a gate in the bushes. "The gardens are through there. You can play in all of them, except one that's locked up.

Mr. Craven shut it when his wife died ten years ago and buried the key."

A bell rang, and Martha hurried away. Alone, Mary stepped outside, left to wonder about the locked garden.

# CHAPTER 4

## Gardens and a Gardener

Mary went through the little gate into a big garden. It had wide lawns and winding paths, trees, flowerbeds, and an old gray fountain. But everything was bare, and there was no water in the fountain.

At the end of a path, she came to a wall with a green door. It opened into another walled garden. Another open door led to yet another walled garden. Mary didn't know that these were kitchen gardens for growing fruit, vegetables, and herbs. They were certainly ugly in the middle of winter, she thought.

She was still exploring when an old man came through one of the doors. He carried a spade over his shoulder. He didn't seem at all happy to see Mary.

In her quite sharp voice, she asked, "What is this place?"

Gruffly, he answered, "A kitchen garden. There's another beyond that door, and an orchard on the other side of that."

"Can I go play in them?" Mary asked.

"If you want, but there's nothing to see."

Mary turned away and walked to the next green door. She entered a garden with beds of winter vegetables, some covered by glass frames. She found another wall with a green door, which was closed. Could it be the garden that no one had entered for ten years? Mary grabbed the door handle, hoping it wouldn't open.

But the handle gave way. She entered an orchard of bare fruit trees. Walls surrounded the orchard, but no more doors. She noticed that one wall seemed to go beyond the orchard. Maybe it led to something on the other side?

On a treetop behind the wall, a robin red-breast was perching. He burst into his winter song.

Mary perked up. The bird's friendly little whistle made her feel better, and she almost smiled. When he flew away, she wondered if she would see him again. Perhaps he lived in the mysterious locked garden.

Mary was very curious about the locked garden. If Mr. Craven had loved his wife, why did he hate her garden?

She walked back to the first kitchen garden and crept up on the old man, who was digging.

"I visited the orchard," she reported. "But there's no door to the garden on the other side of the wall," she said crossly. "I did see a bird with a red breast in a treetop singing."

The old man began to whistle, and then Mary heard a little rustle. A bird flew over to them. He perched on a clod of dirt near the gardener's foot. It was wonderful.

The old man stopped digging. He asked the bird, "Where've you been, you cheeky little fellow? Have you begun courting this early in the year?"

The bird hopped and pecked the ground for seeds and insects. He seemed sprightly and cheerful, and Mary started to feel the same way as she watched him.

"Does he always come when you whistle?" she asked.

"Aye," the gardener said. "I've known him since he was a chick. He flew over from the other garden. But he was too weak to fly back for a few days. That's when we got friendly. He's a robin redbreast. They're the friendliest, most curious birds alive. See? He knows we're talking about him. He's a stuck-up one," the gardener chuckled.

"Where's his family?" Mary asked.

"Don't know. When he was strong enough to fly back to his nest, his brood had gone. But he's smart—he knew he was lonely, and he flew back to me."

Mary took a step nearer the robin and looked at him very intently. "I'm lonely," she confided. Until then, she had only felt cross but didn't know why.

The gardener stared at her. "Coming here from India—it's no wonder," he said. Then he began to dig again.

"What is your name?" Mary asked.

"Ben Weatherstaff," he said. "I'm lonely, too, except when he's around. He's my only friend."

"I've never had a friend," Mary said.

"You and me are a good bit alike," Ben Weatherstaff said. "We both have faces like sour pickles. And we both act as sour as we look. Same nasty tempers, I guess."

No one had ever spoken so plainly to Mary. She wondered if she really did look as sour as he said.

A clear, rippling sound broke through her thoughts. The robin had flown into an apple tree nearby and was singing.

Old Ben laughed. "He wants to make friends with you."

Mary looked up at the robin. In a voice as soft and eager as any child's, she said. "Would you make friends with me? Would you?"

"You said that so nice and human!" Ben exclaimed. "Almost like Dickon when he talks to the wild creatures on the moor."

"Do you know Dickon?"

"Everybody knows him."

Mary wanted to know more, but just then the robin spread his wings and flew away.

Mary watched him go. She cried out, "He's flown into the garden with no door!"

"He lives there," Ben said. "Maybe he's courting some lady robin who lives in the old rose trees."

"Are there roses in the garden?" Mary asked. She had seen roses in India.

"There were ten years ago," Ben mumbled to himself.

"Where's the door?" Mary asked.

"Nowhere anyone can find," Ben said roughly. "And it's nobody's business. Don't you go poking your nose where it doesn't belong! Get on now and play. I've got work to do."

Then he hoisted his spade onto his shoulder and trudged away.

CHAPTER 5

# A Cry in the House

❧

For a while, every day was like Mary's first. Martha would bring her breakfast and help her dress. Mary would complain more than she ate. Then she'd go outside to explore the gardens.

But after several days, she woke up feeling hungry. "It tastes nice today," she said of her porridge.

"It's the fresh moor air that's given you an appetite," said Martha. "You keep playing outdoors. It'll soon put flesh on your bones and color in your cheeks."

"I have nothing to play with," Mary replied.

"You've got sticks and stones!" Martha exclaimed. "My brothers and sisters play with what they can find. They run and shout and look at things."

Mary did look at things in the gardens. Sometimes she saw Ben Weatherstaff, but he was always too busy to pay attention to her.

She discovered a long walkway outside the garden walls, where thick ivy grew. Mary found a place at the end of the walkway where the ivy was extra thick and bushy. She wondered why it had not been trimmed like the rest.

One day she was staring up at a long tendril of ivy swinging in the wind. Suddenly she saw a flash of red—the robin redbreast perched atop the wall.

"Oh!" she cried out. "Is it you?" It didn't seem odd to talk to him. He twittered and chirped back. To Mary, it seemed that he was saying "Good

morning!" and inviting her to come along with
him.

Mary laughed. She ran after him as he hopped
and took short flights. "I like you!" she cried out.
She made chirping sounds and tried to whistle,
and the robin seemed pleased. He flew up to a
treetop to sing, behind the orchard wall on the
other side of the garden.

"He must live in the garden without a door!"
she thought.

She ran up the path and back through the
kitchen gardens to the orchard. She went straight
to the wall where she had first seen him. There he
was—just finishing his concert.

"It *is* the secret garden," she said to herself. "I
am sure it is!"

She searched again for a door in the orchard
wall, but still found nothing. So she ran all the
way back to the long path that wound along the

ivy-covered wall. She walked up and down, searching very carefully. Still, no door.

That night, Martha chatted amiably while Mary ate. Mary didn't mind listening to her now.

When Mary finished her supper, she and Martha sat near the fireplace. The wind was howling outside. It banged at the windows like an invisible giant trying to break in. But by the fire, they felt safe and warm.

Mary asked, "Why did Mr. Craven hate the garden?"

Although hesitant, Martha tried to explain.

"It was his wife's, and she loved it. Mr. and Mrs. Craven tended the flowers themselves. None of the gardeners ever went in. The two of them would stay there for hours, just reading and talking. In it was an old tree with a branch that bent like a seat—Mrs. Craven liked to sit there. But one day, the branch broke and she fell. She was hurt so badly that she died the next day. That's why Mr.

Craven hates it. Mrs. Medlock says nobody can talk about it, or about lots of other things . . . "

Mary fell silent. She was thinking about Mr. Craven and how sad he must be, when just then she heard a curious sound, like a child crying. She was sure that it was coming from inside.

"Do you hear that?" she asked.

Martha looked confused. She said, "It's the wind. Sometimes it sounds like someone's lost on the moor, crying for help."

"But it's here," Mary insisted, "down one of the corridors."

At that instant, a strong gust blew open Mary's door with a crash. The light went out. The sound of crying grew louder than ever.

"I told you!" Mary shouted. "Someone is crying, and it isn't a grown-up!"

Martha jumped up. Then they both heard a door somewhere being banged shut.

"It must be the new kitchen maid crying,"

Martha said stubbornly. "She has an awful toothache."

Mary stared hard at Martha. Inside she knew that Martha was not telling the truth.

# CHAPTER 6

# Opening Doors

౼ఞ

It rained the next day, and the moor almost disappeared into the gray mist. Mary would not be able to go outside.

"What does your family do when it rains?" she asked Martha.

"Mostly we try to keep from getting under each other's feet," Martha chuckled. "The older children play in the cowshed. But Dickon goes out like it was a sunny day. Once he found a half-drowned fox cub and brought it home. Another time he found a young crow and named it Soot because it was so black. Now it goes with him everywhere."

"If I had a fox or a crow, I could play with it," Mary said.

"Can you read? You could read a book or work on your spelling," Martha suggested.

"I can, but all my books were left in India," Mary said.

Martha had an idea. "There are thousands of books in the library. Mrs. Medlock might let you in."

But Mary had another idea.

When Martha left, Mary stood at her window and thought of a plan. She didn't care much for the library, but it reminded her of the hundred rooms with closed doors. Were they all locked? What was inside them? If there really were a hundred, she could count them. At least it would be something to do.

She quietly left her room and entered a long

hallway that branched off into other ones. There were doors everywhere and pictures on the walls. She wandered into a long gallery. Its walls were covered with paintings of men and women in grand costumes of satin and velvet.

Mary continued to explore. One room down the hall seemed to be a lady's sitting room with embroidered velvet covering the walls. A little cabinet displayed dozens of little elephants made of ivory. Mary had lived in India, so she knew all about elephants.

She played with the ivory elephants until she grew tired and decided to return to her room, but she had lost her way. She came to a tapestry hanging at the end of a short hallway.

As she tried to decide which way to go, a cry broke through the stillness. It wasn't like the crying she had heard the night before: this time it was a short, childish whine.

Her heart began beating fast. "It *is* crying," she said to herself, "and it's nearer than last night!"

She brushed against the tapestry by mistake. To her surprise, she opened a hidden door. Mary could see down another hall, and at the end of it, Mrs. Medlock coming toward her carrying a bunch of keys. She looked very cross.

"What are you doing here?" Mrs. Medlock demanded. She took Mary's arm and pulled her away.

"I took a wrong turn—" Mary began, "and then I heard someone crying—"

"You didn't hear anything of the sort," Mrs. Medlock snapped. "Go to your room now, or I'll box your ears!"

Mrs. Medlock pulled Mary down the twisting hallways back to her room.

"Stay where you're told or you'll be locked in!" the housekeeper warned sharply.

Then she left, slamming the door. Mary sat by the fireplace. She was furious, but she didn't cry. She thought about what she'd discovered that morning: the maze of rooms, the ivory elephants, and the crying—someday, she would discover who it was.

CHAPTER 7

# A New Discovery

∽

Two days later, the weather cleared. For the first time, Mary could see the moor in full sunlight. The sky was unlike any she'd ever seen—it was a sparkling deep blue. Small white clouds dotted the sky. The moor looked softly blue, not the dreary purple-gray that Mary was used to.

Martha explained, "The colors are beautiful this time of year. The storms go away for a while because spring is on the way."

"I thought it was always rainy and dark in England," Mary said.

"Not at all!" Martha laughed. "Yorkshire can be the sunniest place in the world. Just wait till the wildflowers bloom! Hundreds of butterflies flutter in the air. The bees hum and the skylarks sing—you'll want to be on the moor all day, just like Dickon. I wonder what Dickon would think of you," Martha said, smiling.

"He wouldn't like me," Mary replied in her cold tone. "Nobody does."

"But do you like yourself?" Martha inquired kindly, as her own mother had asked her when she was in a bad mood.

Mary didn't answer for several moments. Then she said, "Not really—not at all. But I never thought about it before."

After Martha left, Mary felt lonelier than ever.

Mary hurried to the garden and ran around the old fountain ten times. She counted each lap and felt better when she had finished. She looked up again at the blue sky and tried to imagine lying on a fluffy white cloud and just floating. Then she went into one of the kitchen gardens, where Ben Weatherstaff and two other gardeners were working.

Old Ben said to Mary, "Springtime's coming. Can you smell the good, rich earth?"

Mary sniffed. She thought she could smell something fresh and damp. She thought that the good weather had made Ben warmer, too.

Mary was watching Ben dig when she heard a soft rustling. The robin alighted on the ground. He was very lively and hopped all around her feet.

"He's never known a little girl before," Ben said. "He wants to find out all about you."

"Are things growing where he lives? In the garden with the old rose trees?" Mary asked.

"Ask the robin," Ben said. "He's the only one who's been inside it for ten years."

A little later, Mary wandered off. She was

thinking of how she liked the garden, and how she'd begun to like the robin, and Dickon, and Martha's mother, and Martha. She wasn't used to liking people.

She found the path outside the ivy-covered wall. The robin flew around there, too. He hopped about the bare flowerbeds, pecked at the ground, and pretended not to notice Mary. But she knew that he had followed her. This excited her.

"You are the prettiest bird in the world!" she exclaimed, "and you remember me!"

Mary talked and chirped back to him; the robin puffed out his chest, flicked his tail, and twittered. She put her face close to his and tried to make robin sounds. But she knew not to touch him for fear of frightening him away.

The robin hopped over to the flowerbed and began to peck for a worm. Then Mary noticed something in the dirt: it looked like a rusty ring of iron or brass. She waited until the robin flew back to a treetop. Then she reached down.

But it wasn't a ring. It was an old key, and it had been buried for a long time.

# CHAPTER 8

# Something in the Ivy

Mary put the key in her pocket. She decided to keep it with her whenever she went outside, in case she found the hidden door to the garden. She wouldn't ask for permission to go in, either. She imagined making a special place just for herself.

As she thought, she stared at the ivy walls. "It's very silly," she said tartly. "I'm so near the garden, but there's no way in!"

The next morning, Martha returned from her day off with lots to tell Mary.

"I told my family about you!" Martha said

cheerfully. "They wanted to hear all about the little girl from India who had been waited on her whole life."

Mary said, "I'll tell you more before your next day off. Your brothers and sisters might like to hear about riding on elephants and camels and hunting tigers."

"My word!" Martha exclaimed with delight. "That would be as good as the wild animal shows!"

She then put her hand into her apron pocket.

"I've brought you a present," Martha said. She took out a strange object: a rope with a striped handle at each end.

Mary was mystified. She'd never seen one and asked what it was for.

"It's a skipping rope," Martha explained. "Mother bought it from a peddler. Just watch!"

Martha went to the middle of the room and began to skip. She counted to a hundred. When she stopped, her cheeks glowed and her eyes sparkled. Her breath came in little pants.

"I could already skip to five hundred when I was twelve," Martha said breathlessly. She handed the rope to Mary. "Now you try," she said. "It does take practice, but Mother says there's no better toy. She says that skipping rope will stretch your limbs and make you stronger."

Mary wasn't very good at skipping. Still, she liked trying and didn't want to stop.

"Go skip outside," Martha said. "Mother says you should be outdoors as much as you can."

Mary got into her coat and slung her new toy over her arm. She was about to leave when she turned back to Martha.

"It was your wages that bought this rope, wasn't it? Thank you, Martha."

She said it so stiffly because she wasn't used to thanking people. Then she held out her hand.

Martha shook it. The handshake was a little formal, but Martha understood that

Mary wasn't used to showing her feelings.

Outside, Mary began to skip rope while counting. She skipped around the fountain, then into the kitchen garden.

Ben Weatherstaff was there with the robin. "Well!" he declared. "Perhaps you are a youngster—not an old lady with sour buttermilk in her veins!"

"I can only skip to twenty," Mary said, "but I'm getting better."

"You keep on going," Ben said. "That robin will want to see you, I'm sure."

So Mary skipped into the orchard. She wasn't used to so much exercise, but the more she skipped, the easier it became. At last, she reached the path beside the ivy wall.

The robin was perched on a long branch in the thickest part of the ivy, chirping overhead.

Mary laughed at him. "You showed me the key yesterday," she called out, "but I don't believe you can find the door!"

Then something happened that could only have been magic.

A gust of wind blew down the path: it was pleasant and strong. It blew some of the ivy branches away from the wall. They stirred like window curtains in a breeze.

Mary grabbed the loose ivy. She had seen something in the wall—a round doorknob hidden by the vines. Her heart thumped in her chest. She held the ivy away from the door. Touching the door with her fingers, she felt a small hole—a keyhole.

Trembling, she took the rusty old key from her pocket where she had been hiding it. She put it in the keyhole. She had to use both hands to turn it, but somehow it did turn.

She glanced up and down the path. No one was coming, so she took a deep breath and pushed. Very slowly and creakily, the door opened.

She slipped inside and shut the door behind her. She was now inside the secret garden.

# CHAPTER 9

## Such a Strange Place

The garden was the most mysterious place anyone could imagine. Its walls were covered with
bare branches. Wintry brown grass covered the
ground. There were clumps of bare bushes and little trees. Mary knew that they were rose plants
like she had seen in India.

There were other kinds of trees. The climbing
rose canes hung down like curtains, and the vines
had grown together, making little bridges
between the trees. The tangle of branches and
vines made the garden seem so mysterious.

It was very quiet. Even the robin in the tree-top didn't move.

In a whisper she said, "I am the first person to speak in this place in ten years!"

She walked over the brown grass. Stopping under one of the vine bridges, she wondered if they were all quite dead. She hoped not.

Even so, she was inside the garden: a world of her own at last. The sun was shining, and the sky looked even bluer here. The robin flitted from one tree to the next. He chirped busily, telling her about the garden. She forgot to feel lonely. She kept thinking how beautiful it would be if the garden came alive.

She began to skip around the garden, taking it all in. There were little paths in the grass, stone benches, and moss-covered urns. Then she noticed a flowerbed full of dried grass with little green shoots sticking out of the ground.

She remembered what Ben had told her.

"There *are* things growing here!" she exclaimed. "It isn't quite dead!"

She looked about carefully. She found many more pale green shoots among the old beds.

Although she had never been a gardener, she thought she could help tend the little plants. She found a sharp stick. With great care, she dug away the grass around a few plants. She dug up some little white things that looked like onions and then replanted them.

When she'd cleared a space, she said, "Now the plants can breathe." She decided to do more each day until she had done them all.

Mary almost forgot about lunch and had to run back to the house. Martha was very surprised to see Mary's rosy cheeks and bright eyes. She was even more surprised when Mary asked for double helpings of meat and rice pudding.

While eating, Mary asked, "What are those white things in the ground that look like onions?"

"They're bulbs," Martha said. "The little ones are snowdrops and crocuses. The bigger ones are daffodils, and the biggest are lilies and irises. Those flowers live a long time—they spread out and have little ones. Dickon planted bulbs all around our cottage."

"Does Dickon know about flowers?" Mary asked.

"Our Dickon can make flowers grow on a stone wall," Martha said with pride. "Mother says he just whispers things out of the ground."

Mary finished her pudding and went to sit by the fireplace.

"I wish I had a little spade," she said.

"Whatever for?" Martha asked.

Mary didn't want to give away her secret. If

Mr. Craven found out, she feared, he might lock up the garden forever.

After a minute she said, "I don't have much to do here. I only have you and Ben Weatherstaff to talk to, and you're both so busy. If I had a spade and some seeds, I could make a little garden."

Martha's face lit up. "Why, that's what Mother said! You could grow parsley and radishes."

"Your mother knows so many things, doesn't she?" Mary said.

"She says that a mother who raises twelve children learns more than the ABCs," Martha chuckled. "Now, I've seen little garden sets at the shop in Thwaite. There's a spade, a rake, and a fork that cost but two shillings."

"I have that!" Mary almost shouted. "Mrs. Medlock gives me a shilling every week."

Martha said, "If we write Dickon a letter, he

can buy the tools. And some flower seeds, too. Can you print?"

Mary nodded eagerly.

"I have some chores to do for Mrs. Medlock," Martha said, "but I'll come back as soon as I can with some paper and a pen and ink."

So Mary didn't get to go back to the garden that day. When Martha returned much later, together they printed a nice letter to Dickon and Martha signed it.

"Put your money in the envelope. Dickon will buy your tools, and he can bring them to you."

"Then I shall meet the boy who tamed foxes and crows!" Mary exclaimed.

Martha stayed with Mary until suppertime. When Martha got up to fetch Mary's supper, Mary asked shyly, "Does the kitchen maid have another toothache today?"

Martha looked uncertain. "Why do you ask?"

"Because I heard crying again down the

corridor. That's three times now—and there wasn't any wind today."

Martha looked uneasy. She said, "You must not go walking about the halls—Mr. Craven would be very angry!" Then she hurried away before Mary could say another word.

Mary thought, "This is the strangest house ever!"

# CHAPTER 10

# Dickon

⟡

Mary called her special place the "secret garden." In it she felt like part of a fairy story. She had read about people who went to sleep in secret gardens for a hundred years. But instead, Mary was becoming wider awake.

She could run faster and longer now and skip to a hundred. Every day she worked in the garden to give the bulbs breathing room. Mary was oddly stubborn when something interested her, and the garden interested her more than anything she had ever known.

She learned more about gardening from Ben. And he usually welcomed her company. In fact, he was flattered that she wanted to talk to an old man. Also, Mary no longer spoke to him as if he were a mere servant.

One day he paid her a gruff compliment. "You're starting to be a credit to Misselthwaite," he said. "You're not so thin and pale. You looked like a plucked crow when you first came here."

Mary liked old Ben and even his homespun honesty. One day he told her why he especially liked roses. "I was gardener to a young lady who had a rose garden, and she loved her roses like they were children. That was ten years ago," he sighed. "But the lady's in heaven now, and the roses are overgrown. I tried tending them— pruning them a bit and digging around the roots—but my stiff old body makes it too hard."

Thinking of the secret garden, Mary asked, "When roses have no leaves, and they look grayish brown and dry, how can you tell if they're still alive?"

"In the spring, look for little bumps on the twigs and branches. Watch 'em after a warm rain and see what happens."

He stopped digging suddenly and stared at Mary. "Why do you ask?" he said crossly. "Girls shouldn't ask so many questions. Go off and play—I've got work to do."

She wasn't mad at being sent away. She liked Ben even when he was cross with her.

Mary walked away from Ben and found the path that curved around the secret garden. It was lined with laurel hedges and ended at a gate opening into the woods. She hoped to see rabbits there, but instead she heard a whistling sound coming from the other side. Curious, she followed it into the woods.

What she saw took her breath away: a boy sitting under a tree with rust-colored hair, cheeks as red as poppies, and the roundest, bluest eyes Mary had ever seen. He was playing a pipe, and a squirrel was clinging to the tree just over his shoulder. A pheasant behind a small bush stretched its neck to peek out at him. Nearby sat two rabbits twitching their noses as if they had come to a concert.

When the boy saw Mary, he raised his hand. In a low voice he said, "Don't move! It would frighten them."

He stopped playing and stood up very slowly—almost like he wasn't moving at all. When he finally got to his feet, the animals scampered away. They didn't seem afraid.

"I'm Dickon," the boy said, "and *you're* Miss Mary."

He talked in a friendly way. But Mary felt shy around boys. "Did you get our letter?" she asked rather stiffly.

Dickon nodded his head yes. "I've brought the

garden tools." He showed her a package wrapped in brown paper. "There's a spade, a rake, a fork, and a hoe. A trowel, too, and some extra seeds. The woman at the store threw in a packet of white poppy and blue larkspur for free."

"Can you tell me about the seeds?" Mary asked, opening the package. The way he talked sounded as if he liked her. She forgot about being shy.

They sat on a log, and Dickon explained all about the seeds and how to plant them.

They heard chirping coming from a holly bush. "There's a robin calling us," Dickon said. "He's calling someone he's friends with."

"He's Ben Weatherstaff's robin," Mary said. "I think he knows me a little."

Dickon whispered, "He's telling me he likes you!"

Dickon moved quietly to the bush. He made a

sound like the robin's own twitter. The robin answered.

Mary was amazed. "Do you really understand everything birds say?" she asked.

Dickon grinned. "I think so," he said. "I've lived on the moor so long that I feel I'm one of them. Sometimes I think I'm a bird or a fox or a badger."

He laughed and came back to the log. Then he asked, "Where is your garden? I can help you plant."

Mary turned red and then pale. She twisted her hands in her lap and looked at the ground.

Dickon was puzzled. He asked, "You do have one, don't you?"

Mary said nothing for several minutes. Then she looked up and said, "Can you keep a secret? It's a great one. If anyone found out, I think I might die!"

Dickon was more puzzled than ever. But he said in a good-natured way, "I keep secrets all the time. I keep the animals' secrets so no one bothers them on the moor."

Mary grabbed his sleeve and spoke very fast. "I've stolen a garden! Nobody wants it, and maybe it's all dead, but I don't care! Nobody can take it from me!"

Then she threw her arms over her face and burst into tears.

Dickon drew out a soft "Oooooh!"

Mary wiped at her tears. She said, "I found it myself and got in myself, like the robin. They wouldn't take the garden away from a robin!"

"Where is it?" Dickon asked.

Mary jumped up. "I'll show you," she said.

Dickon followed her through the gate, up the laurel path, and to the ivy-covered walkway. He didn't speak, but looked kindly at her.

Mary found the door and led him inside.

"It's a secret garden," she said. "They're letting it die—but I want it to live!"

Dickon took his first look around. In a curious whisper he said, "It's a strange, pretty place. It's like we're in a dream!"

# CHAPTER 11

## A "Wick" Garden

‿∽

For several minutes, Dickon just looked around. Then he started walking about the gray trees and twisting vines, the overgrown grass, and the stone seats and urns.

"We used to wonder about this place," he said softly. "Just look at the tangle—this must be the safest nesting place in England! No one could bother the birds up there."

"Will there be any roses?" Mary whispered.

Dickon stepped over to the nearest tree. He

took a knife from his pocket and cut into a branch.

"There's lots of deadwood, but it's as wick as you and me," he told her. Grinning widely, he showed Mary a little brownish green shoot.

"Wick?" she asked.

"That's Yorkshire for 'alive,'" Dickon said.

"Oh, I'm glad it's wick!" Mary exclaimed.

Dickon put a finger up to his lips.

Mary whispered happily, "I want everything here to be wick!"

One shrub at a time, Dickon showed her how to cut away the deadwood to find the living wood. "When it looks greenish and juicy, it's wick. When it's dry and breaks off easy, you cut it away." Then he showed her how to dig around the roots to let the plants breathe.

There was so much to do that Mary asked if Dickon could come again and help.

"I'll come every day if you want," he offered. "We'll wake up this garden. You'll get stronger, and I'll teach you to talk to the robin. We'll have loads of fun!"

He looked around again and said, "But I don't think the garden should be *too* neat. It will look nicer with things running a bit wild."

Mary agreed that it wouldn't seem like a secret garden if it was too tidy.

"Hmm. It looks like someone did some pruning and digging not too long ago," he noted.

"But the door was locked, and the key was buried. How could anyone get in?" Mary said.

Dickon scratched his head. "Aye, how could it be?" he murmured.

They kept working in the warm sunshine. Mary was startled when the clock in the courtyard chimed twelve, time for lunch.

Dickon had brought a sandwich to eat in the

garden and work some more before going home. Mary hated to leave. She was afraid Dickon would disappear like a wood fairy.

Walking to the door, she turned and said, "Whatever happens, you—you would never tell about the garden?"

Dickon smiled. "If you were a thrush and you showed me your nest, do you think I'd tell? Not me. Your secret is safe."

# CHAPTER 12

## Just a Bit of Earth

෴

When Mary ran into her playroom, Martha was waiting.

"I've seen Dickon!" Mary exclaimed. "He brought the garden set!"

Martha had never seen the girl so excited. She asked, "Where is your garden to be?"

Mary couldn't tell her about the secret garden, so she said, "I haven't got one yet."

"Um," Martha said. "If I were you, I'd talk to Ben Weatherstaff. He'll find a place for your garden."

Mary ate her lunch hungrily so she could hurry back to the garden and Dickon. But when she finished, Martha had some important news. Mr. Craven had come home and asked to see his niece.

"But why?" Mary asked. Her face grew pale. "He didn't want to see me before."

"It's because of Mother," Martha said. "She saw him in Thwaite village, and she spoke to him. He's leaving again tomorrow for Europe and won't be back till next fall."

This made Mary feel better. If Mr. Craven went away, she'd have time to see the secret garden come alive.

Mrs. Medlock opened the door in her best dress, looking a bit nervous. She told Mary to change her clothes and brush her hair. Then she took Mary to a part of the house she had never seen.

They entered a large room where Mr. Craven

was sitting in an armchair before the fire. He thanked Mrs. Medlock and dismissed her. Mary was surprised to see that he wasn't a hunchback, although he had crooked shoulders.

"Come here," he said.

Mary stood before him. He had dark eyes and black hair streaked with white. He wasn't ugly and could have been handsome if he didn't look so unhappy.

"Are you well?" he asked. "Do the servants take good care of you?"

"Yes," she answered.

"You are very thin."

"I'm getting fatter," Mary said in her stiff way.

Mr. Craven rubbed his forehead. "I intended to get you a nursemaid or a governess."

"Oh, please—no—" Mary stammered. "I'm too big for a nurse. And don't make me have a governess yet!"

Mr. Craven looked away. To himself he said, "The Sowerby woman said she needs to get stronger before she has a governess."

Mary heard the name and asked, "Is that Martha's mother?"

"Yes," he replied. "Mrs. Sowerby said you should play outdoors and get sturdier."

"She knows all about children," Mary said.

"Yes. Mrs. Craven was very fond of her," he said. His voice softened when he mentioned his wife. "Now, tell me where you play."

Mary gasped out, "Everywhere. I run and skip, but I don't do any harm!"

"Don't look so frightened." He sounded worried. "You may do what you like. I'm your guardian, though a poor one for a child. I can't give you much attention, but I want you to be happy and comfortable. Is there anything you want? Toys, books, dolls?"

Mary's voice trembled. She said softy, "Might I have a bit of earth?"

Mr. Craven looked startled. "Earth? What do you mean?"

"A place to plant seeds—make them grow—watch them come alive," Mary said. "When I was in India," she explained, "I was always too ill and it was too hot, but here it's different."

Mr. Craven stood up and crossed the room. He seemed to be deep in thought. When he spoke to her again, his eyes looked soft and kind.

"You can have as much earth as you want," he said. He remembered his wife's love of things that grow. "When you see a bit of earth you want," he smiled, "you may take it, child. Make it come alive."

Then he rang the bell for Mrs. Medlock.

Mr. Craven spoke to the housekeeper. "This child needs to be stronger before she begins to have lessons," he said. "Give her simple, healthy food. Let her run in the garden, but don't look after her too much."

Mrs. Medlock looked relieved. Mary could be quite a handful.

"Mrs. Sowerby is to come here sometimes, and Mary may visit the Sowerbys' cottage."

Back in Mary's room, Martha was waiting with a surprise.

"I can have my garden!" Mary cried happily. "Your mother can come to see me, and I can visit your cottage! Mr. Craven really is kind."

Martha was as delighted as Mary. She helped her change into her play clothes, and Mary ran outside. She hoped Dickon would still be in the garden, but he had gone. His tools lay neatly under a tree. Only the robin remained.

A piece of paper fastened to a thorn on a rosebush caught Mary's eye. It was the letter she'd sent to Dickon. On the back was a drawing that looked like a bird's nest and some printed words: "I will come back."

# CHAPTER 13

## A Mysterious Boy

Thats a picture of a thrush nesting," Martha said when Mary showed her the note.

Then Mary understood: the garden was a nest, and she was like a thrush. Dickon would keep their secret.

She looked forward to seeing Dickon the next day, but during the night, she awoke to the sound of rain beating at her window and the wind roaring.

She sat up in bed, feeling angry. "The weather is as contrary as I am!"

She tossed and turned for about an hour. Then she heard something fretful. She sat up again and listened.

It wasn't the wind—it was crying. Mary made up her mind to find out who it was. She got out of bed and put on her robe and slippers. She lighted a candle and headed down the long and dark hallway. Mary was too excited to be afraid. She remembered the way to the door behind the tapestry where Mrs. Medlock had been so angry to find her.

The crying grew louder as she approached it, down some passages and up a few steps.

She pushed the tapestry aside and opened the hidden door. The crying was clearer now. She saw a faint light under another door and went in.

She found herself inside a big room with handsome furniture and a hearth fire. A candle flickered on a table beside a big four-poster bed. On it lay a boy crying pitifully.

She crept forward. Her bright candle attracted the boy's attention.

"Are you a ghost?" he asked in a half-frightened voice.

"No," Mary whispered. "Are you?"

He stared at her with big gray eyes that looked too large for his thin face.

"I'm Colin Craven," the boy said.

"I'm Mary Lennox. Mr. Craven's my uncle."

"He's my father," the boy said.

Mary was stunned. "No one told me he had a boy!" she gasped.

"Come closer," Colin said. He put out his hand and touched her.

"You are real," he said softly. "I thought you were one of my dreams." Colin sat up. "Where did you come from?" he asked.

"My room. Didn't anyone tell you that I live here?"

"They wouldn't dare," he said. "They know that I won't let people see me."

"Why not?" Mary asked.

"Because I'm ill. I was born too soon, and if I live, I'll probably be a hunchback. But I probably won't . . . I don't like people to see me and talk about me. My father only comes when I'm asleep. He doesn't want to see me, either."

"Why not?" Mary asked. It was all such a mystery.

"My mother died when I was born. He does-n't think I know, but I hear people talking—he almost hates me and wishes I were dead."

"Don't you ever go outside?" she inquired.

"Never. I used to be taken to the seaside in my wheelchair, but people stared at me. I had to wear irons on my legs. A doctor from London said I needed fresh air, but I hate fresh air. I can't stand people gawking at me."

Mary asked if she should go away, but Colin motioned her to sit next to him on a big stool. He wanted to know more about her.

"Everybody here has to do what I want," he said as if it were normal. "They can't make me angry because I probably won't grow up."

Then he asked, "How old are you?"

"Ten," she said, "just like you. When you were born, your father locked the garden and buried the key."

This got Colin's attention. His eyes grew

larger. "What garden? Why did he lock it?" he demanded.

Mary felt nervous. She thought, "He hates the garden because his wife died." Out loud she said, "It's the garden your father hates. No one has been inside it for ten years. Nobody is even allowed to talk about it."

"I can make them talk," Colin declared. "If I were to live, Misselthwaite would be mine. They'd have to tell me."

This comment scared Mary. If he asked questions, what might happen? She changed the subject. "Do you really think you won't live?"

"I don't suppose I will," he replied crossly. "I don't really want to live, but I don't want to die. When I'm sick, I think about it all the time. It makes me afraid and I cry."

He paused. "But about the garden—I could *make* them open it!"

Mary twisted her hands in anguish.

She cried out, "Don't do that! If they open the garden, it will spoil everything! If we could find it—if no one could go there but us—don't you see? It would be our secret."

Colin lay back on his pillows. "I've never had a secret before."

"I'm sure I can find the garden," Mary went on. "Then you could go there. Maybe we could find a nice boy to push your wheelchair."

"I'd like that," he said in a dreamy kind of voice.

Mary felt a little safer. She began telling him about the other gardens and about Ben Weatherstaff. Colin smiled when he heard about the robin.

After a while he said, "I want to show you something."

He pointed at a curtain that hung above the mantel and told Mary to pull the cord. Behind the curtain was a painting of a laughing girl. Her dark hair was tied with a blue ribbon, and her gray eyes looked just like Colin's.

"That's my mother," he said with disgust. "I don't know why she had to die. If she'd lived, maybe I wouldn't be sick. Maybe my father wouldn't hate to look at me." He turned away and ordered Mary to close the curtain. "I don't like her to look at me."

Again Mary asked if she should leave. She was afraid that Mrs. Medlock might find her.

"I won't allow Medlock to be angry at you," Colin said. "I'm glad you're here, and I want this to be our secret. I'll tell Martha whenever I want to see you. She stays with me when my nurse is away."

Then he said quietly, "I wish I could go to sleep before you leave."

Mary pulled the footstool closer. "I can sing

for you like my Ayah used to sing for me. Just close your eyes."

Mary sang him an Indian lullaby she'd learned as a baby while stroking his hand. "That is nice," Colin said, as he drifted off to sleep.

Mary crept away softly.

# CHAPTER 14

## Colin the Rajah

❦

Martha was very busy the next day. It was afternoon before Mary could talk to her.

"I've found out who was crying last night," Mary said, "and I went to his room. It's Colin."

Martha looked red with fright. "You shouldn't have done that!" she said tearfully. "You'll get me in trouble!"

"It's all right," Mary said. "He was glad I came."

"Are you sure?" Martha asked. "When he's angry, he screams and throws the most terrible tantrums to frighten us."

"He wasn't angry at me. We talked, and he showed me his mother's portrait. Then I sang him to sleep."

Martha was amazed. "It's like you walked into the lion's den! He never lets strangers look at him. But if Mrs. Medlock finds out, she'll say I told you, and she'll send me away!"

"Colin wants it to be our secret. He wants you to tell me when I can go and see him. Mrs. Medlock will have to obey him."

Then Mary asked what was wrong with Colin.

Martha had calmed down a bit. She began, "No one really knows. He began all wrong with his mother dying and his father raging with grief. The doctors were afraid Mr. Colin had a weak back, so they kept him lying down all the time. He had to wear an iron brace."

"He's very spoiled," Mary said, not realizing that she had been spoiled, too.

"Well, he's had many colds and coughs,"

Martha said. "He had rheumatic fever once, and typhoid. Mother says all he needs is fresh air and running around, but he just lies in his room reading picture books and taking medicine. The last time he went out, he began sneezing. A new gardener looked at him, and Mr. Colin threw a terrible tantrum, yelling, 'He thinks I'm a hunchback!' Then he cried himself into a fever."

"If he gets angry with me, I won't see him again," Mary said.

"He'll see you if he wants," Martha smiled. "He always has his way."

A bell rang, and Martha got up. "His nurse wants me to watch him for a while," she said. "I hope he's in a good temper."

She returned ten minutes later. "Well, you have bewitched him!" she said in amazement. "He's sitting up, and he wants you to come as quickly as you can."

Mary hurried to Colin's room. In daylight, she

saw how beautiful it was. The walls and rugs were richly colored, and the fire burned brightly. Colin's cheeks glowed in his pale face.

"Martha's scared," Mary told him. "She thinks Mrs. Medlock will send her away if she finds out we've met."

Colin frowned. "Tell Martha that everyone has to do what I please, and that I will send Medlock away if she gets angry when she brings you. I'll take care of everything," said Colin regally.

Mary looked at him oddly. "I was just reminded of a boy I once saw in India," she began. "He was a rajah—that's a royal prince. He talked to his people just like you do. They had to do whatever he said—they might have been killed if they didn't."

She paused. "I was also thinking how different you are from Dickon, Martha's brother. He's twelve years old, and he can charm the birds and foxes and squirrels with his pipe, just like an Indian *fakir* or snake charmer."

Colin was curious to hear more. Mary told him how Dickon knew all the creatures that lived on the moor.

"But how can he like the moor?" Colin asked. "It's such a dreary place."

"On the night I arrived," Mary said, "I hated it, too. But Martha talks about it, and Dickon tells me it's a beautiful place full of living things."

"I wish I could see it," Colin said, "but I can't go out because I'm going to die. Everybody says so."

Mary didn't like the way Colin almost boasted about dying. She said in her most contrary way, "If everybody wished me to die, then I wouldn't do it! Besides, I don't believe everybody thinks you'll die. The doctor from London didn't. He made them take off the irons."

"That's true," said Colin. "One time I heard

him say, 'The lad might be fine if he makes up his mind. Put him in a humor to get well.'"

Mary said, "Dickon could do it. He talks about living things—not about being sick and dying."

Colin was enjoying himself so much that he forgot about his weak back. He sat up straight and said, "I just thought of something. Did you know we're cousins?"

They were both in a mood to laugh.

Suddenly Mrs. Medlock entered with Dr. Craven, a cousin of Colin's father.

"What's the meaning of this?" the doctor said in alarm.

In his best rajah voice Colin said, "This is my cousin Mary Lennox. She must be allowed to come whenever I send for her."

Mrs. Medlock wailed, "Who let her come in here?"

"Nobody," Colin said. "Mary heard me crying, and she came by herself."

Dr. Craven sat down and took Colin's pulse. "It's fast, my boy," the doctor said. "Excitement is not good for you."

"I will get more excited if she doesn't visit me," Colin said, staring at the doctor. "She makes me feel better. I want her to stay for tea." He commanded Mrs. Medlock to bring some tea and snacks. She hurried off to carry out his order.

The doctor finally agreed to let Mary stay. He also left, shaking his head in disapproval.

When Mrs. Medlock brought their refreshments, Colin helped himself to a hot muffin and offered one to Mary. He said, "Now. Tell me all about rajahs."

# CHAPTER 15

## Nest Building

꩜

It rained for the whole next week. Mary missed going to the garden and seeing Dickon. But she and Colin spent hours talking, playing games, and reading to each other. He hadn't had a crying fit since he met Mary.

Mary was very cautious about talking to Colin of the secret garden in case he couldn't keep a secret. But how could they get him there without anybody knowing? She was sure the garden would help him get better as it had helped her.

At the end of the week, Mary woke up very early. Outside the sky was blue again. She jumped out of bed and ran to open her window. A sweet, fresh breeze greeted her. She put her hand out the window to feel the sun.

"It's warm!" she thought. "It will make the sprouts grow and the bulbs work very hard. Oh, I must see the garden now!"

She dressed quickly to the sound of birds singing. She hurried downstairs to a small side door she could unlock by herself. Outside, the grass had turned green and there seemed to be living things in every bush and tree. Little shoots were sprouting in every flowerbed and border. The world was waking up.

She ran to the secret garden. She was about to fling open the door when she heard a strange "caw caw." Looking up, she saw a big, blue-black bird on top of the ivy-covered wall. It made her nervous, and she hoped it would fly away.

When she entered the garden, the crow flew to an apple tree. Under the tree was a small reddish animal with a bushy tail, and Dickon kneeling in the grass.

As Mary approached, the animal went over to Dickon. The crow flew down and perched on his shoulder.

Dickon introduced his companions. "This fox cub is Captain. The crow here is Soot. They followed me across the moor this morning."

The fox and crow stayed with Dickon as he and Mary walked around the garden. They didn't seem afraid of Mary.

Mary told Dickon how she had met Colin and played with him every day. "He says I make him forget about being ill and dying," she whispered.

"I'm glad you know about him," Dickon whispered back. "I couldn't have told you myself."

Mary was surprised. "What do people know about Colin?"

"Folks know he's ill," Dickon said. "They know Mr. Craven doesn't want him talked about, and can't bear to see his son when he's awake. Mr. Colin reminds him of his wife."

"Does Colin really want to die?" Mary asked.

"No, but Mother says he wishes he'd never been born, and that's the worst thing for a child to think."

Mary said softly, "Mr. Craven is afraid Colin will grow a hunchback. Colin's so afraid, he almost never sits up. He feels his back for lumps. He says if he ever finds one, he'll scream himself to death."

"He'll never get well if he keeps thinking like that," Dickon said, rubbing the fox's neck. "If Colin were here, he wouldn't think about finding lumps. He'd watch the buds break out and the flowers bloom. Do you think he'd be willing to come here?"

"I'm sure he would," Mary said. "He knows about the garden, but not that we've found it. Maybe he'd come outside for us. He could order the gardeners and everyone to stay away. I'm certain Colin could keep a secret."

Dickon smiled. "Then we'll get him out for sure."

CHAPTER 16

An Argument

⟋

Mary had almost forgotten about seeing Colin that afternoon. After lunch, she asked Martha to tell him that she couldn't come till later.

"That will put him in a bad mood," Martha said fearfully.

But Mary wasn't used to thinking of others' feelings. She didn't understand how lonely life could be for a person who was ill and nervous and thought he couldn't control his temper.

She and Dickon worked all afternoon. They rested a little, and Dickon played a song on his flute. He told her about the trees that would bloom before spring was over—apple, cherry, peach, and plum. As the sun set, they both promised to return to the garden the next morning.

When she returned, Martha was waiting. Her face was not happy.

"Mr. Colin's been acting terrible all afternoon," Martha said. "We've had quite a time keeping him quiet. You should have gone to see him today."

But Mary didn't feel guilty or afraid when she went to his room. She marched straight up to him and said, "Why are you still in bed?"

"I got up this morning thinking you were coming," he said, looking away, "but I made them put me in bed this afternoon. My back and my head ached. Why didn't you come?"

"I was in the garden with Dickon," she said.

"I won't let him come here anymore," said Colin in his rajah manner.

Mary grew angry, stiff, and stubborn. "If you send Dickon away, I'll never visit you again!"

"I'll make you!" he shouted. "They'll drag you here!"

"Oh, will they, Mr. Rajah?" Mary said fiercely. "But they can't make me talk to you! Or look at you!"

Even though they couldn't have a rough-and-tumble fight, they could yell and shout.

"You're selfish!" Colin cried.

"No—you're selfish!" Mary shouted.

"I'm not as selfish as Dickon!" Colin yelled. "He keeps you playing in the dirt when he knows I'm here all alone."

Mary's eyes flashed with anger. "Dickon's nicer than any other boy!" she exclaimed. "He's magical! He's like—an angel!"

"He's just a common country boy," Colin said with a sneer.

"He's better than a common rajah!" Mary shouted back.

Their arguing was getting the better of Colin. He'd never had a fight with anyone who argued back. So he turned his head away and cried a little tear of self-pity.

"I'm not selfish," he whimpered. "I'm ill. I have a lump on my back, and I'm going to die soon..."

"You are not," Mary said frostily.

"But I am! Everybody says so!" Colin cried.

"I don't believe it," Mary said sourly. "You say that to make people sorry for you. You're proud of it."

At that, Colin was so angry that he forgot his aching back and sat straight up.

"Get out of my room!" he screamed. He threw his pillow at her. It landed at her feet.

Mary went to the door. She stopped to say, "I was *going* to tell you all sorts of nice things—about Dickon's fox cub and his crow—but now I won't tell you a single thing!" And she stormed out.

Walking back to her room, Mary felt cross. She was thinking that she wouldn't tell Colin about the secret garden. It would serve him right!

Then she remembered how afraid Colin was that he would become a hunchback and die. She knew he had tantrums when he was tired and afraid.

"Just maybe he was thinking about lumps because he was alone this afternoon," she thought. "I think I will go see him tomorrow— even if he throws pillows at me."

# CHAPTER 17

A Tantrum

But Mary didn't see Colin the next day. Instead, she worked in the garden till sunset. She was very tired and went to bed soon after supper. She decided to see her cousin the following afternoon.

In the middle of the night, dreadful noises awoke her. She heard doors slamming and someone crying and screaming horribly.

"It's Colin," she said. "He's having hysterics!"

Just listening made her feel sick and shivery. She pressed her hands to her ears, but the noise was too loud. She wanted to have a tantrum her-self—to frighten Colin as much as he was fright-ening everyone else.

Mary hurried to Colin's room. The closer she got, the louder were his screams. She slapped open his door and ran to his bed.

"You stop!" she shouted. "I hate you—every-body does! You'll scream yourself to death in a few minutes, and I wish you would!"

She went on. Her words were just the shock Colin needed. He was lying on his stomach, jumping around like a caught fish. His face was red and swollen as he gasped and choked.

But Mary didn't care.

"If you scream again, I'll scream louder than you!" she shouted.

"I can't stop!" he wept. "I felt a lump on my back!" Then he turned over and sobbed some more. But he didn't scream.

"No you didn't," Mary said fiercely. "If you felt

something, it was an imaginary, hysterical lump. Let me look."

She called to the nurse, "Come show me his back this minute!"

The nurse, Mrs. Medlock, and Martha all huddled in the doorway. The nurse seemed afraid to touch Colin, but he gasped in fear, "Sh-show her! Then she'll see!"

The nurse gently pulled down Colin's night-shirt to expose his spine. Colin was pitifully thin, and his ribs showed. Mary examined his back with her most solemn expression.

"There's not a single lump," she proclaimed at last. "Nothing but backbone. You can feel it because you're so thin. But there's not a lump as big as a pin. If you ever say it again, I'll just laugh!"

No one had spoken to him this way before. The adults didn't know about his secret fear, and he had never known other children who might have told him the truth. Now Mary was so angry and cross that he almost believed her.

The nurse said, "I didn't know he thought he had a lump. His back is weak from disuse, but there's no lump."

"There isn't?" Colin asked with a sob.

"None at all, sir," the nurse replied.

"Do you think—I could—live to grow up?" For a change, Mary heard him speak like a real boy, not like a rajah.

The nurse told him what the London doctor had said. "You probably will if you do as you're told, control your temper, and get plenty of fresh air."

Colin felt worn out, and became gentler. Mary, too, was not angry anymore.

He put out his hand for her to take.

"I'd like to go out with you," Colin said. "I won't hate fresh air if we can find—" He stopped himself: he'd almost said "the secret garden."

Then he said, "I'd like to go out if Dickon would push my chair. I'd like to meet Dickon and his animals."

The nurse brought the children cups of tea, and Mrs. Medlock and Martha slipped away. The nurse told Colin that he needed to sleep but that Mary could stay for another half hour.

When the nurse had gone, Colin squeezed Mary's hand. "I almost told them about the secret garden," he said anxiously, "but I stopped myself. Have you found a way in yet?"

Mary looked into his red, swollen eyes. "Yes," she said softly, "I think I have. If you go to sleep, I'll tell you everything tomorrow."

"Won't you tell me what you *imagine* it looks like?" Colin begged. This was better than picture books. "You can pretend you've seen it."

Colin's eyes were already heavy, so Mary talked him to sleep. She told him how the rose vines *might* climb over the walls and hang from tree branches and how daffodils and snowdrops *might* be growing underground. She told him how the birds *might* build their nests there, where it was safe and quiet . . .

Colin very happily fell asleep.

# CHAPTER 18

## Sharing a Secret

୦ଡ଼ଡ

Mary slept late into the next morning.

Martha awoke her and said, "Colin is feeling ill after his tantrum, but he asked, 'Please see if Miss Mary will come talk to me.' Imagine him saying 'please'! Will you go?"

Mary agreed.

She was wearing her hat when she went into Colin's room.

"Are you going somewhere?" he asked in a weary but pleased voice.

"I have to talk to Dickon, but I'll be back

soon," she said. "It's—about the secret garden."

Colin's eyes lit up. "Oh, I dreamed about it last night!" he remarked. "I'll keep imagining it until you come back."

Five minutes later, Mary was in the garden. Dickon was working, with two squirrels called Nut and Shell sitting on his shoulders. Captain lay on the ground, and Soot perched on a tree branch.

Mary told Dickon her idea that he

could visit Colin the next day with the animals. After a few days, they could bring Colin outside.

"Aye, a good plan," Dickon agreed.

Mary wanted to stay in the garden, but she knew Colin was waiting. She hurried back to his bedside, where Colin did a strange thing. He sniffed at her.

"I smell flowers and fresh things," he said. "It's cool and warm and sweet at the same time."

"Aye, lad," she said just like Dickon would, "it's the wind from the moor and the smell of new grass in springtime."

Mary talked to Colin about Dickon and his animals. She told him about Soot and Captain and the two squirrels. She described the wild pony that followed Dickon across the moor.

"Does the pony really understand Dickon?" Colin asked.

"It seems like magic," Mary replied, "but

Dickon says that anything will understand you if you're friends with it for sure."

"I've never had anyone to be friends with," Colin said sadly, "and I can't bear other people."

"What about me?" Mary asked.

"Oh, I like you," Colin said.

"I used to not like anybody," Mary admitted, "but I got to know Ben and the robin and Dickon. I probably wouldn't like you if I hadn't liked them first."

"I wouldn't mind Dickon looking at me," Colin said.

"I'm glad," Mary answered, "because . . ."

Then she told him about the plan for Dickon's visit, about finding the key and the ivy-covered door, and about their work to make the secret garden grow.

"Oh, Mary," he said with a kind of sob, "will I live to go in and see it?"

"Of course you will!" Mary snapped. "Don't be silly."

Colin relaxed and laughed at himself.

Then Mary said, "I couldn't tell you about the garden before because I was afraid. But now I trust you for sure!"

CHAPTER 19

Colin's Visitors

୧ର

Dr. Craven came to Misselthwaite Manor as
always after one of Colin's tantrums. He expected
to see a pale, weak, sobbing boy lying in bed.
Imagine his surprise when he saw Colin sitting up
on the sofa and reading a picture book with Mary.

"Er, I'm sorry to hear that you were ill," the
doctor said nervously.

"I'm much better today," said Colin the rajah,
"and I plan to go outside in a day or two for some
fresh air."

"I thought you didn't like fresh air," said the doctor, taking Colin's pulse.

"I don't when I'm alone," Colin replied royally, "but my cousin is going with me, and a very strong boy I know will push my wheelchair."

Colin slept soundly that night and woke up smiling, stretching his arms and legs. His mind was full of plans and thoughts about the garden and Dickon and his wild creatures. It was nice to have good things to think about.

"Dickon says spring has come!" Mary cried joyfully, bounding into his room.

Colin had stayed indoors for so many years that he didn't really know about seasons changing.

"Open the window," he said happily. "Maybe we'll hear golden trumpets announcing that spring has come!" He had read about such fanfare in storybooks.

Mary opened the window. "Lie on your back

and breathe in the air. That's what Dickon does when he's on the moor. He says it makes him feel strong—like he could live forever and ever."

Colin took in big, deep, sweet breaths.

After a while, the nurse arrived with breakfast for the children. She was setting their places when Colin made his announcement.

In his best rajah voice he said, "A boy, a fox, a crow, and two squirrels are coming to see me this morning. I want the servants to bring them here. The boy is Martha's brother Dickon: he's an animal charmer."

Soon after, Colin heard a "caw-caw" in the hallway.

"It's Soot!" Mary said.

Martha opened the door and said, "If you please, sir, here's Mr. Dickon and his creatures."

Dickon came in grinning widely. A crow sat on his right shoulder and a squirrel on his left. Another squirrel peeked out of his pocket.

Captain trotted beside him. And in his arms, Dickon cradled a baby lamb.

Colin stared in speechless wonder. He'd never spoken to another boy before, let alone a menagerie. But Dickon wasn't at all shy. He knew that creatures stare until they find out about you. So Dickon didn't say anything at first. He went over to Colin and lay the baby lamb in his arms.

The lamb nuzzled against Colin's side.

"What is it doing?" Colin asked.

"It's hungry, and it wants its mother," Dickon explained.

He knelt down beside Colin and took a feeding bottle from his pocket. The woolly baby began sucking on it happily.

By the time the lamb fell asleep, Dickon had told Colin all about finding the little creature on the moor.

As Colin and Mary listened, Soot flew in and out of the open window. The squirrels scampered

onto the sill and explored a big tree outside. Captain curled up comfortably at Colin's feet.

Dickon and Mary told Colin more about the garden and all that was growing there. Colin's eyes grew huge with excitement.

He exclaimed, "I'm really going to see it!"

"You will," Mary said. "And there's no time to lose."

# CHAPTER 20

# Going Outside

⌒

One day the children gathered in Colin's room to plan how Colin could go to the secret garden without anyone else finding it. When they had decided on a plan, Colin summoned Mr. Roach, the head gardener. Mr. Roach was alarmed because he'd heard stories about the boy's terrible temper and princely ways. He feared he might be ordered to cut down oak trees or dig up orchards.

When he entered, Colin's room was full of animals. Colin sat in an armchair, holding court.

"I have some important orders for you," Colin

said to Mr. Roach. "I'm going outside. If the fresh air agrees with me, I may go out every day. When I'm out, the gardeners are to work in the greenhouses until I say they can go back outside."

Mr. Roach was relieved. "Very well, sir," he agreed.

That afternoon, the strongest footman at Misselthwaite carried Colin downstairs. The nurse helped Colin into his wheelchair, surrounded by cushions with a blanket over his legs. Then Colin waved all the grown-ups away. Dickon pushed the chair outdoors slowly, and Mary walked beside it.

At last they came to the long path by the ivy-covered walls.

"This is where the robin flew over the wall," Mary said in a soft tone. She pointed at a spot under a lilac tree and said, "And that's where I found the key."

They reached the place where the robin had

perched in the ivy. "This is where the wind blew back the ivy," Mary explained.

She held back the thick ivy to reveal the garden door. She turned the handle, and Dickon pushed Colin forward.

Colin covered his eyes until they were inside. The door clicked shut. Colin dropped his hands and took his first look at the secret garden.

All around he saw the tender green vines and branches of the rose plants. Overhead bloomed the white and pink puffs of blossoms in the fruit trees. Dotting the ground were gold and purple and white flowers. The air was full of chirping and birdsong. The sun felt warm on his face.

Mary and Dickon both stared at Colin. There was a pink glow in his ivory face, neck, and hands.

Colin took a deep breath. "I shall get well!" he shouted with glee. "Mary! Dickon! And I shall live forever and ever!"

# CHAPTER 21

Someone Else in the Garden

꼬

Dickon pushed Colin around the garden. Colin wanted to hear about every tree, flower, and blade of grass. Sometimes he laughed at Dickon's stories and Mary had to remind him to speak softly.

They finally stopped under the apple tree. Colin noticed something new. "That old tree over there," he inquired, "is it quite dead?"

"Aye," Dickon said. "But the roses have climbed over it. When the flowers bloom, it'll be the prettiest in the garden."

"It looks like a big branch has broken off," Colin remarked. "I wonder how that happened."

Mary felt uneasy because she didn't want her cousin to know about his mother's accident. She was relieved when the robin distracted Colin by darting over to its nest with a fat worm in its beak.

Colin chuckled softly. "He's taking an afternoon snack to his mate. I could use some tea and biscuits myself."

Maybe the garden was magical, Mary thought. Colin seemed like a completely different boy. His face glowed, and he laughed; it was as though nothing could make him angry or afraid.

"I don't want this afternoon to end," Colin said, "but I'll come back tomorrow and the day after, and every day after that. I'll see spring and summer here. I'll watch everything grow—I'll grow here myself!"

Dickon said, "We'll have you walking and digging before long."

Colin's face flushed. "You think so?"

Dickon answered cautiously, "Well, you've got legs, same as other folks."

Mary was nervous until Colin said, "There's nothing really wrong with them, except they're very weak and thin. I'm afraid to stand because they shake so much."

"You'll stop being afraid after a while," Dickon smiled.

They were all quiet for some time. They wanted to enjoy every last minute of the afternoon. But their silence was broken when Colin said in an alarmed whisper, "Who's that man?" while pointing to the high wall. Mary and Dickon instantly turned around.

It was Ben Weatherstaff on a ladder, peering down at them.

He shook his fist at Mary. "I should have known it was you! You're a bad one—always poking your nose where it doesn't belong!"

Mary called back, "It was the robin who showed me the way!"

This made old Ben madder. "Don't you be blaming the robin!" he bellowed. Then his curiosity got the best of him and he asked, "How did you get in?"

Before Mary could reply, Ben saw something coming across the grass: it was Colin in his wheelchair. Ben's jaw dropped in astonishment.

"Do you know who I am?" Colin demanded.

Ben was so shocked, he could hardly speak. He hadn't seen Colin since he was a baby and had only heard the stories people told. At last Ben said without thinking, "Aye, I know you. You have your mother's eyes. You're the poor crippled lad!"

Colin's face turned beet red. He sat up and yelled, "I am not a cripple!"

"You don't have crooked legs?" Ben asked in a hoarse voice.

This was too much for Colin. His anger and pride made him forget everything else. He threw the blanket off his legs and called to Dickon for help. Colin grabbed Dickon's arm, stuck out his thin legs on the grass, and stood up—tall and straight as an arrow.

"Look at me!" he shouted.

What Ben did next was even more surprising to Mary. The old man choked and gulped, and tears ran down his wrinkled cheeks.

Ben gasped out, "You're as thin and white as a ghost, but there's not a bump on you. Bless you, boy—you'll be a man yet!"

Colin stayed standing. In his rajah voice he said, "When my father's away, you have to obey me. This is my garden. Get down from that ladder—Miss Mary will show you inside. Now that you've seen us, you'll have to keep our secret."

Ben could hardly take his eyes off the boy. Then he touched his hat politely and said, "Yes, sir!"

Mary ran out of the garden. Colin turned to Dickon, who was beaming. "I told you that you could stand up when you stopped being afraid!" he grinned.

Colin held his head high. Then he remembered what Mary had said about Dickon. "Are you doing magic?" he asked.

"No, *you're* doing the magic," Dickon replied. "The same magic that makes plants grow and trees blossom."

"I want to walk to that tree," Colin said, "so I will be standing there when he comes in."

And he did it. Dickon held his arm, but Colin was wonderfully steady. He was standing beside the tree when Mary and Ben entered. Mary was amazed. Under her breath, she repeated, "You can do it!"

Colin addressed Ben, "Look at me! Am I a hunchback? Have I got crooked legs?"

"Not you, sir," Ben said in almost his usual way. "But why have you been hiding—letting folks think you're crippled and half-witted?"

"Who said that?" Colin demanded angrily.

"Lots of folks tell lots of lies," Ben said.

"Everyone said I was going to die," Colin said fiercely, "but I'm not!"

Ben looked him up and down. "No so," he said gently. "You've got too much pluck. I saw that when you planted your feet on the ground. Now sit yourself down a bit, sir."

Colin did sit. In a softer tone he asked what work Ben did in the gardens.

"Anything I'm told," the old man said. "I'm kept on here because your mother—she liked me." There was a soft look in his eyes. "This was her garden. After she was gone, I'd come here in secret and climb over that wall. But the last two years, I haven't been able to—because of my stiff knees."

"So *you* did the cutting and pruning!" Dickon exclaimed.

Ben continued, "Mrs. Craven was so fond of this place. Once she made me promise that if she was ever ill or away, I'd tend her roses. When she died, everybody was ordered to stay out, but I kept my promise."

"I'm glad you did," Colin said kindly, "and I know you can keep our secret."

"Aye, I will," Ben said. "And I'll be glad to come in by the door again."

Colin reached for Mary's trowel. His hand was

weak, but he stuck the trowel in the ground and turned over some dirt. He looked up at Dickon and said, "You told me I could walk and dig. And here I am doing it!"

Ben laughed hoarsely. "You're a Yorkshire lad for sure," he said. "How'd you like to plant something? I can get a rose in a pot."

Colin gladly agreed, and Ben hurried away, forgetting about his aches and pains. With Dickon's help, Colin dug until the hole was deep enough.

Ben soon returned from the greenhouse. He hobbled as fast as he could and presented the potted rose to Colin. Colin set the plant in the hole and held it while Ben filled in the soil firmly.

"I planted it!" Colin proclaimed with satisfaction. "Help me up, Dickon. I want to be standing when the sun sets—that's part of the magic."

When the sun went down on this strange and wonderful day, Colin was standing straight up on his own two feet and laughing.

# CHAPTER 22

# The Magic

Everything that happened in the garden seemed magical: the plants grew, the seeds took root, and the children changed for the better. Ben would talk to them about gardening and about Colin's mother. "She loved plants that could almost touch the sky. She said the blue sky always looked so joyful," he shared.

One day Colin told Mary, Dickon, and Ben to stand in a row. "I'm going to try a scientific experiment," he announced grandly. "I'm going to discover all about magic—just like scientists study electricity. Mary knows about it because she's from India where they believe in magic. Dickon is an animal charmer. I learned to stand up here. So each day, I'm going to say, 'Magic is in me. Magic is making me well. Magic is making me as strong as Dickon.' Will you help me by saying the words?"

"What should we do?" Mary asked. It seemed rather mysterious.

Colin had them sit in a circle. He began to chant. Over and over he said, "Being alive is the magic. Being strong is the magic. The magic is in me. It's in all of us!"

After some time Colin announced, "Now I'm going to walk around the garden."

He led the way. Dickon walked on one side and Mary on the other, followed by Ben, the squirrels, the fox, and the lamb. Every few yards they stopped to let Colin rest. Colin held on to Dickon's arm, but managed a few steps alone. He kept repeating his chant until he had circled the whole garden.

"I did it!" he cried. "The magic worked. My first scientific discovery!

"Dr. Craven mustn't know," Colin warned. "No one can know until I can walk and run like other boys. I'll keep coming here and back in my wheelchair. But when my father returns to Misselthwaite, I'll walk into his study and say, 'Here I am, like any other boy! I'm well, and I will live to be a man!'"

"He won't believe his eyes," Mary said happily.

"After my experiment is over," Colin told them, "I'm going to become an athlete."

Ben almost jumped up with excitement. "We'll teach you to box. You can be the champion prizefighter of England!" he declared.

Colin was quick to correct him. "I shall not be

a prizefighter. I shall be a scientific discoverer."

Ben humbly pulled his cap down and said, "I beg pardon, sir." But under his cap, Ben's eyes twinkled with delight. He knew the boy was gaining in strength and spirit.

# CHAPTER 23

## Susan Sowerby Saves the Day

The children had agreed that Mrs. Sowerby could share their secret. Dickon told his mother how Colin and Mary were getting plumper and rosier every day. But there was a problem: the servants at the manor couldn't find out that Colin was regaining his health.

"He and Miss Mary have to do some playacting," Dickon said with a grin. "Mr. Colin complains as usual and acts helpless, and Miss Mary treats him like he's a weak, pitiful thing. When they get to the garden, they burst out laughing."

Mrs. Sowerby nodded. "Good healthy laughter's better than pills any day."

Dickon said, "They're both so hungry now that they keep asking for more food. But if they ask for too much, the servants and the doctor get curious. The doctor said that he'd write to Mr. Craven about it, which scared Colin. Colin wants to surprise Mr. Craven when he comes back."

"Maybe I can help," Mrs. Sowerby said. She offered some fresh milk, extra bread, and currant buns for Dickon to take to the garden.

The next morning, Dickon surprised his friends with two tin pails: one filled with rich, creamy milk and the other containing fresh buns wrapped in a checkered napkin. The children were grateful for the delicious food and ate hungrily.

Colin remarked, "Mrs. Sowerby must have the magic in her, too, that makes her think of ways to do nice things."

Now staying inside on rainy days made Colin

bored and restless. One dreary day, Mary invited Colin to explore the mysterious old house with its hundred rooms that nobody went into.

"A hundred . . ." Colin said dreamily. "That's as mysterious as a locked garden!"

They both laughed.

They played in the room with the little ivory elephants and explored rooms Mary hadn't seen, new hallways, staircases, pictures, and strange old things.

Back in Colin's room, they ate every bite of lunch. Mary also noticed something odd in his room: the curtain no longer covered the picture of his mother above the fireplace.

Colin noticed and said, "I like to see her now. One night I woke up and saw moonlight shining on the curtain—it was like magic filled the room. I opened the curtain, and it was as though she was laughing because she was glad to see me standing up."

Mary looked at the picture and said, "You look so much like her now—like her ghost made into a boy."

"If I look like her, then maybe my father will be fond of me," he said hopefully.

# CHAPTER 24

# Homecoming

⤳

While the secret garden was coming alive, a lonely man with crooked shoulders was visiting beautiful sights in Europe. But nothing made an impression on his gloomy heart.

After months of travel, Mr. Craven was staying at an inn near a mountain stream in Austria. One day he walked out by himself. Sitting beside the stream, he watched the birds fly down to drink. Clusters of blue forget-me-nots were growing beside the softly rushing water. For the first time in ten years, he felt himself relax and notice how lovely everything was. Slowly, new and beautiful thoughts began to push out his old, sad ones.

He began to come back to life.

That autumn, he traveled to Italy. One warm night, he was sitting beside the lake near his hotel. The full moon was reflected in the water. Everything was so calm that he fell asleep.

He dreamed that he was in a place filled with roses. A distant voice called out his name: it was his wife's. In the dream he cried out, "Where are you?"

The sweet voice answered, "In the garden!"

He slept till dawn. When he awoke on the ground, he could still hear her words echo, "In the garden!"

A servant handed Mr. Craven a bundle of letters and went away. The one on top from Yorkshire caught his attention.

He read it at once, and then again. It said:

*Dear Sir,*

*I once spoke to you about Miss Mary. Now I must speak again. Please, sir, you must come home. I think you would be glad to come. If I might be so bold, I think your wife would ask you to come if she was here.*

*Your obedient servant,*

*Susan Sowerby*


He thought about the letter and about his dream. He decided to return to England at once.

On the train back to Yorkshire, he worried that Colin was seriously ill, maybe dying. But he decided not to give in to his dark thoughts anymore. For the first time in years, he looked forward to coming home. His heart felt warm.

When he finally reached the manor, he called for Mrs. Medlock and asked how his son was.

"To tell the truth," Mrs. Medlock said, "Mr. Colin might be better or he might be changing for the worse. We can't make him out. You know how he hated to see people and would never go outdoors. Well, he's taken a great fancy to Miss Mary and Dickon Sowerby. Now they push him in his chair and go outside by themselves every day. None of us is allowed near them. I've tried to protect him, but he's there now, sir—in the garden."

Her words rang in his ears: they were the same sweet words of his dream.

He left Mrs. Medlock to go find his son. He followed the same route Mary had taken on her first day at the manor. He knew where he must go, but he walked slowly. It had been so many years since he locked the door to his wife's garden, he wasn't sure if he could find the key.

When he reached the ivy-covered wall, he stopped and looked around. He heard a scuffling sound as if someone was running in the autumn leaves. He seemed to hear voices—and the happy laughter of children. Was he dreaming?

Suddenly, the door of the locked garden flew

open. A boy burst through it, running at full speed. The boy didn't see the man and nearly crashed into him.

Mr. Craven grasped the boy to keep him from falling. Who was he? Mr. Craven saw that he was tall and handsome. His cheeks glowed and his thick, curly hair fell over his forehead. The boy's eyes shone with laughter when he pushed his hair back. Mr. Craven gasped when he saw the gray eyes, rimmed with black lashes and full of boyish fun.

Colin had not planned to meet his father this way. But this was better. He'd been running a race and had dashed through the door ahead of Mary. Now he was standing with his father's hands on his shoulders.

"I'm Colin," he said. "You can't believe it. I can hardly believe it myself!"

Mr. Craven could only repeat, "In the garden!"

Colin exclaimed, "Yes, Father! The garden did it. And Mary and Dickon and the wild creatures. And the magic. We kept it all secret until you came. I'm well now! And I'm going to be an athlete and a scientific discoverer!"

Colin spoke so naturally that Mr. Craven trembled with joy. He looked into his son's handsome, healthy face. He was speechless.

Finally, Mr. Craven said, "Take me into the garden, my boy. Tell me all about it."

The garden was brilliant with autumn colors—gold and purple, violet, and flaming red. Late lilies of white and red waved in the breeze. Autumn roses climbed upward and hung like curtains from the yellowing trees. Mr. Craven remembered when they were planted.

"I thought it would be dead!" he gasped.

"Mary thought that when she found the garden," Colin said, "but it came alive."

The children led Mr. Craven to the grassy spot

under their tree. They introduced Dickon, and everyone sat down. Colin and Mary began to tell their story. It was the strangest tale Mr. Craven had ever heard. Sometimes he laughed so hard that tears came to his eyes. And sometimes his cheeks were wet just like old Ben's when he saw Colin stand up.

Ben had been listening nearby. He excused himself so that he could be back at the house when the servants first set eyes on Mr. Craven and Colin.

When Ben entered the kitchen, Mrs. Medlock asked if he had seen Mr. Craven or the boy.

"Aye," Ben said. "I've seen them both."

"Together?" Mrs. Medlock asked anxiously. "What did they say to each other?"

"I couldn't tell," Ben replied with a sly grin, "but there's things going on outside that you house people don't know."

He went over to the kitchen window.

"Well, look at that," he said. "Look what's coming across the lawn!"

Mrs. Medlock looked out the window. She threw up her hands and screamed in surprise. The cook, Martha, and the other servants ran over and stared out the window in amazement.

Across the grass came the Master of Misselthwaite, smiling and laughing like no one had ever seen before. And at his side walked a tall, smiling lad as straight and steady as any boy in Yorkshire. The servants gasped—it was Master Colin!

## What Do *You* Think?
### Questions for Discussion.

∽

Have you ever been around a toddler who keeps asking the question "Why?" Does your teacher call on you in class with questions from your homework? Do your parents ask you questions at the dinner table about your day? We are always surrounded by questions that need a specific response. But is it possible to have a question with no right answer?

The following questions are about the book you just read. But this is not a quiz! They are designed to help you look at the people, places, and events in the story from different angles. These questions do not have specific answers. Instead, they might make you think of the story in a completely new way.

Think carefully about each question and enjoy discovering more about this classic story.

1. At the beginning of the story, Mary always did whatever she wanted and had no friends. Why do you think she acted this way? What advice would you have given her?

2. Mrs. Medlock tells Mary that her uncle is "not going to bother about you," and that she will have to look after herself. How does Mary react to this? How would you feel if you were Mary?

3. Martha asks Mary if she likes herself. What do you think she meant by that? Do you ever have times when you don't like yourself?

4. Loneliness makes people behave differently. How are each of the characters affected by their loneliness?

5. Do you think the robin could really understand what Ben and Mary were saying? Do you believe that animals have special powers? Did the robin actually lead Mary to the key to the secret garden?

6. How do you imagine the secret garden looks?

7. Mary says that Dickon "talks about living things—not about being sick and dying." Why do you suppose this kind of attitude is important?

8. Colin says, "Magic is in me. Magic is making me well." Do you believe in magic? Who or what is the source of the magic that is making Colin healthy?

9. In what ways are each of the children like the garden? Is Mr. Craven like the garden?

10. Have you ever dreamed of discovering a secret garden or room or land of your own?

# Afterword

*by Arthur Pober, EdD*

ᢙ

First impressions are important.

Whether we are meeting new people, going to new places, or picking up a book unknown to us, first impressions count for a lot. They can lead to warm, lasting memories or can make us shy away from any future encounters.

Can you recall your own first impressions and earliest memories of reading the classics?

Do you remember wading through pages and pages of text to prepare for an exam? Or were you the child who hid under the blanket to read with a flashlight, joining forces with Robin Hood to save Maid Marian? Do you remember only how long it took you to read a lengthy novel such as *Little Women*? Or did you become best friends with the March sisters?

Even for a gifted young reader, getting through long chapters with dense language can easily become overwhelming and can obscure the richness of the story and its characters. Reading an abridged, newly crafted version of a classic novel can be the gentle introduction a child needs to explore the characters and story line without the frustration of difficult vocabulary and complex themes.

Reading an abridged version of a classic novel gives the young reader a sense of independence and the satisfaction of finishing a "grown-up" book. And when a child is engaged with and inspired by a classic story, the tone is set for further exploration of the story's themes, characters, history, and details. As a child's reading skills advance, the desire to tackle the original, unabridged version of the story will naturally emerge.

If made accessible to young readers, these stories can become invaluable tools for understanding themselves in the context of their families and social environments. This is why the Classic Starts series includes questions that stimulate discussion regarding the impact and social relevance of the characters and stories today. These questions can foster lively conversations between children and their parents or teachers. When we look at the issues, values, and standards of past times in terms of how we live now, we can appreciate literature's classic tales in a very personal and engaging way.

Share your love of reading the classics with a young child, and introduce an imaginary world real enough to last a lifetime.

## Dr. Arthur Pober, EdD

Dr. Arthur Pober has spent more than twenty years in the fields of early-childhood and gifted education. He is the former principal of one of the world's oldest laboratory schools for gifted youngsters, Hunter College Elementary School, and former director of Magnet Schools for the Gifted and Talented for more than 25,000 youngsters in New York City.

Dr. Pober is a recognized authority in the areas of media and child protection and is currently the U.S. representative to the European Institute for the Media and European Advertising Standards Alliance.

Explore these wonderful stories in our
Classic Starts® library.